WALT DISNEY

Sleeping Beauty

Twin Books

LONGMEADOW
PRESS

Once upon a time, in a faraway land, there lived a king named Stefan and his lovely queen. They were good and kind and were loved by their subjects.

In another kingdom nearby lived their friend, King Hubert, and his son, Prince Phillip. Both kings hoped that one day their kingdoms would be united by the marriage of their children.

For many years King Stefan and his queen had longed for a child. Finally, their wish was granted and a daughter was born. They called her Aurora, which means "sunrise," for she filled their lives with sunshine.

A great holiday was proclaimed throughout the kingdom, so that all might celebrate the infant princess's birth.

People came from everywhere in the kingdom, bringing gifts and good wishes to the Princess Aurora. Ladies in silken gowns, lords in furs and velvet, and knights in bright armor passed through the palace gates. Everyone wanted to see the princess.

King Hubert and his son Prince Phillip were the first to arrive. King Stefan welcomed his friend, and the two kings embraced. They had both waited a long time for this day. Now their children could be betrothed and, when they became of age, could marry. The kingdoms would be united at last.

Young Prince Phillip looked down at the sleeping baby. It was hard to believe that she would one day be his wife.

Then the trumpets sounded as three sparkling balls of light floated into the room. Three fairies magically appeared from the light, waving their wands. They were the three good fairies—Flora, Fauna and Merryweather. They had come to bestow their gifts upon the infant princess.

Flora approached the cradle first. "Little princess, my gift shall be the gift of beauty: gold of sunshine in her hair, and lips that shame the red rose. You shall walk in springtime wherever you go."

Then Flora waved her wand. Flowers of all colors appeared and showered down upon the sleeping beauty.

Then it was Fauna's turn.
"Tiny princess, my gift shall be
the gift of song."
Then she waved her wand
and a chorus of birds flew
above the cradle.

13

At last it was Merryweather's
turn to present a gift to the
baby. The smallest fairy
marched up to the cradle,
waving her wand. "Sweet
princess, my gift shall be…"

But before Merryweather
could continue, a great gust of
wind blew open the doors and
swept into the room. Lightning
flashed, thunder boomed, and
the room filled with darkness.
Suddenly, a bright flame
appeared in the middle of the
great hall. Terrified screams
filled the room.

The flame took the shape of an evil-looking woman dressed in a long black cape. She carried a staff, upon which sat a black raven.

"It's Maleficent!" Fauna gasped. Everyone stood frozen in fear, waiting for Maleficent to speak.

"I really felt quite distressed at not receiving an invitation to your party," Maleficent began, looking at the king. "And to show I bear no ill will, I, too, shall bestow a gift on the child."

She struck her staff on the ground to silence the room before she spoke again.

"Listen well, all of you. The princess shall indeed grow in grace and beauty, but before the sun sets on her sixteenth birthday, she shall prick her finger on the spindle of a spinning wheel…and die."

Everyone gasped in horror.

"Oh, no!" cried the queen. She ran to the cradle and held her baby tight. Maleficent laughed a cruel and heartless laugh.

King Stefan could bear this evil no longer. "Seize that creature!" he shouted.

But before the guards could take her, Maleficent raised her arms and disappeared in a burst of fire and smoke. The raven circled overhead, then flew away, leaving behind a room filled with sadness.

The queen held the princess tightly in her arms. King Stefan tried to console her.

It was Flora who broke the stunned silence. "Don't despair, Your Majesties. Merryweather still has her gift to give."

Merryweather's powers were not strong enough to undo Maleficent's evil curse. But she could soften it.

"Sweet Princess, a ray of hope there still may be in this the gift I give to thee. Not in death, but just in sleep, the fateful prophecy you'll keep, and from this slumber you shall wake, when true love's kiss the spell shall break."

King Stefan was still fearful for his daughter's life. To stop the evil curse, he immediately ordered that every spinning wheel be burned. That night, thousands of spinning wheels were collected and brought to the palace. A large bonfire was lit. King Stefan and his queen felt assured that their daughter would now be safe.

By dawn there was not a spinning wheel left in the kingdom that could threaten Princess Aurora.

But Flora, Fauna and Merryweather knew that this could not stop Maleficent. They had to devise some kind of plan. Flora was the first to come up with an idea.

"Of course the king and queen will object," she said, "but when we explain that it's the only way...."

"We'll disguise ourselves as peasant women and raise Aurora as a foundling child deep in the forest. Maleficent will never expect to find her there!"

Then, with a wave of her wand, Flora turned the other fairies into peasant women to demonstrate her plan.

It was not easy to convince the king and queen of the plan. Sixteen years would be a long time to be without their child. But in the end it was decided that the fairies should take the princess.

One evening, soon after, the three good fairies quietly carried the baby princess away into the night. They would return with the princess just before her sixteenth birthday, when Maleficent's curse would end.

With heavy hearts, the king and queen said good-bye.

And so for sixteen long years the whereabouts of the
princess remained a secret. Deep in a forest, in a woodcutter's
cottage, the good fairies carried out their well-laid plan.
There they raised the princess as their own and they called her
Briar Rose. They never revealed to her anything about the
king, the queen, her royal heritage, or Maleficent.

What is more, the three good fairies lived like mortals. They kept their true identities a secret from Briar Rose and never once used their magic. They cleaned and scrubbed and did everything like common people so Briar Rose would never suspect.

Sixteen years passed quickly and Briar Rose became everything the fairies had bestowed in their wishes. She was not only beautiful, but she was kind. And wherever she went, she carried a song in her heart.

The good fairies knew that soon they would have to return Briar Rose to the castle, where she would resume her rightful identity and marry Prince Phillip.

"Oh, it seems like only yesterday we brought her here," sighed Merryweather.

They would be sad to see it all end. Briar Rose had filled their lives with joy and laughter—things that Maleficent could never understand.

High on the Forbidden
Mountain, Maleficent
continued her search for the
Princess Aurora. For sixteen
years she had sent her goons
throughout the kingdom to
locate the girl, but they could
not find her.

"We searched mountains,
and forests, and houses," the
goon leader said, "and all the
cradles."

It was then that Maleficent realized that for sixteen years they had been searching for a baby.

"Fools! Idiots! Imbeciles!" she screamed. Then she hurled bolts at her goons, just to show her displeasure.

The raven swooped down
and perched himself on the arm
of her throne.

"Oh, my pet," she began,
"you are my last hope. Circle
far and wide. Search for a maid
of sixteen with hair of sunshine
gold and lips red as the rose.
Go, and do not fail me."

The raven flew through the open window and out into the sky. Maleficent knew that the raven would find her princess.

At the cottage in the forest, the three good fairies were busy with plans for Briar Rose's sixteenth birthday party. They wanted it all to be a surprise, so they sent Briar Rose out into the forest to pick wild berries.

Fauna was going to bake the birthday cake and Flora was going to make a special birthday dress. Merryweather was to be the model. Merryweather insisted that they use their magic wands so everything would be perfect.

"No magic," Flora reminded them. They had to keep their identities a secret.

While the three fairies were busy at the cottage, Briar Rose wandered through the forest, picking wild berries. Her friends—the owl, the other birds, the squirrels and the rabbits—joined her. When her basket was full, Briar Rose stopped and sang a song to them. She sang of the man of her dreams.

Her gentle voice carried throughout the forest. Nearby a young prince on horseback heard the lovely voice.

"What is it, Samson?" the prince asked his horse. "Let's find out."

Samson wasn't at all interested. But the prince promised him an extra bucket of oats and a few carrots.

That was all it took. Samson instantly broke into a gallop, carrying the prince closer to the sound of the enchanting voice.

Briar Rose danced and daydreamed while she sang her love song. She did not hear the prince come up behind her. When he joined in singing, she was quite startled!

"I'm awfully sorry," he said. "I didn't mean to frighten you. But don't you remember? We've met before—once upon a dream."

The prince and Briar Rose
danced and sang together. Then
they walked hand in hand
through the forest, as the
animals followed along behind.
It was easy to see that the
two were falling in love.

But when the prince asked her name, Briar Rose realized that she didn't know who he was, either. She had been told never to speak to strangers.

Briar Rose turned to run away.

"But when will I see you again?" the prince called after her.

Briar Rose stopped and answered, "This evening. At the cottage in the glen."

Then she ran off into the forest.

Back at the cottage, the three fairies were in a panic. Fauna looked at the dress Flora had just made.

"Well, it's not exactly the way it is in the book," she said politely.

The cake was in no better shape. It had started to lean to one side. Fauna quickly braced it with a broom. Then the icing and candles slowly slid off the top of the cake and down the broom handle.

"We've had enough of this nonsense," decided Merryweather, all wrapped up in the dress. "I'm going to get our magic wands!" She rushed off to get the wands hidden in the attic.

Quickly, the fairies closed the windows and doors. They
drew the curtains so that no one could see. Then, with a wave
of the magic wands, everything was made perfect.

Flora's dress was a beauty. She directed the ribbon and
scissors in the finishing touches.

Fauna waved her wand at the ingredients for the cake. "Eggs, flour, milk. Just do it like it says," she said to the ingredients, pointing to the recipe book.

In no time at all, Fauna had a beautiful cake prepared.

There was one slight problem, however—the color of the dress. Merryweather liked blue. She waved her wand, and, instantly, the dress turned blue.

But Flora liked pink. With a wave of her wand, she changed the dress back to the color pink.

"Make it blue!" Merryweather insisted. She turned the dress blue again.

Back and forth the colors went. Blue, pink, blue and then pink again. Sparkles flew around the room and up the chimney. The fairies had forgotten to seal off the chimney!

It was just then that the raven flew overhead and saw the colorful sparks coming from the cottage.

He swooped down to have a closer look.

Pink and blue sparks flew from the chimney! The raven knew he had found the princess at last. He flew back to tell the evil Maleficent.

At that moment, Briar Rose returned from her walk in the forest.

"Surprise! Surprise!" the good fairies shouted.

Briar Rose waltzed into the room, hardly noticing the cake or the dress. "Everything's so wonderful! Just wait till you meet him. He's coming here tonight!"

Briar Rose told them about the young man she had met in the forest.

"She's in love," the fairies said sadly. So they decided to tell Briar Rose the truth, that she was really Princess Aurora, and that she was already betrothed to Prince Phillip.

"Tonight we're taking you back to your father, King Stefan," Flora told her.

Briar Rose wept sadly, for she knew she would never see her young man again.

That night the fairies prepared the princess for her return to
the castle.

At dusk they set out for their long journey through the
forest. Princess Aurora hid beneath a long cloak. As she
walked, she thought of the young man she had met that day.
The fairies all thought of that day sixteen years ago when they
had crept thorugh the woods with the infant princess in their
arms.

At the castle, King Hubert and King Stefan were celebrating the upcoming marriage of their two children. They were not pleased when Phillip announced that he was in love with a girl he had met in the forest.

When they reached the castle, the fairies secretly took the princess to a room where they left her alone for a few minutes. But no sooner had they left, than a wisp of light appeared in the room. As if in a trance, Aurora followed the light through a secret panel in the fireplace and up a winding staircase to a hidden tower room. There stood the cruel Maleficent…next to a spinning wheel!

"Touch the spindle! Touch it, I say!" Maleficent commanded.

The three fairies returned to find Aurora gone. Quickly, they followed the path she had taken to the hidden tower. But they were too late. When they arrived at the tower, there stood Maleficent.

"Well, here's your precious princess!" she said with a nasty laugh.

Maleficent stepped back and revealed the fallen princess on the floor. Then the evil fairy disappeared in flames and smoke.

Tears rolled down the cheeks of the three fairies.

"Poor King Stefan and the queen," sobbed Fauna. "They'll be heartbroken when they find out."

"They're not going to," replied Flora. "We'll put them all to sleep until Rose awakens."

The fairies made themselves very small. Then, flying about and waving their magic wands, they put everyone in the castle to sleep—the guards, the royal subjects, even the king and queen.

Just as King Hubert was nodding off to sleep, Flora overheard him trying to tell King Stefan about the peasant girl from the forest Prince Phillip insisted he was going to marry.

Flora put the pieces together and realized that Aurora's young man in the forest was really Prince Phillip. Then she remembered Briar Rose telling them the man would go to the cottage that night.

"Come on," she called to the others. "We've got to get back to the cottage!"

The three good fairies flew as fast as they could to the cottage where Prince Phillip would be arriving, expecting to find Briar Rose. They had no time to lose.

But at the cottage in the glen, Prince Phillip had already arrived. He adjusted his hat, then knocked on the door. A voice from inside asked him to come in. With love in his heart, the prince opened the door and went inside.

Before he realized what was happening, Maleficent's goons jumped on him. The prince was powerless.

The goons tied him up with heavy rope and gagged him with a cloth.

Maleficent stepped out of the darkness and approached the prince.

"Well, this is a pleasant surprise," she said. "I set my trap for a peasant and, lo, I catch a prince. Away with him!" she commanded her goons. "But gently, my pets. I have plans for our royal guest."

Prince Phillip was led away to Maleficent's dungeon.

Again the fairies arrived too late. They found the prince's hat on the ground. They knew at once that Maleficent had been there.

"She's taken Prince Phillip to the Forbidden Mountain!" whispered Flora.

The fairies knew it would be very dangerous to go there, but they also knew they had no other choice. They had to rescue the prince.

At Maleficent's castle, high atop the Forbidden Mountain, Phillip was chained to the dungeon wall.

Maleficent smiled at him. "Oh, come now, Prince Phillip. Why so melancholy?" she asked. Then she proceeded to tell him about Princess Aurora, asleep in King Stefan's castle tower. "But see the gracious whim of fate," she continued. "Why, she is the same peasant girl who won your heart, noble prince, only yesterday."

Maleficent had plans for the prince that would most certainly keep him from rescuing the sleeping princess.

She climbed the stairs to the door with her raven on her arm. "Let's leave Prince Phillip with these happy thoughts," she chuckled.

At that moment, the three fairies flew down from a crack in the dungeon wall. "Shh! No time to explain," they told the prince.

Flora used her wand and struck the shackles off his wrists, while Fauna took care of those on his ankles.

"The road to find your true love may hold still more dangers, which you will have to face alone," Flora said. Then she waved her wand, and a sword and shield magically appeared in Phillip's hands. "So arm yourself with this magic Shield of Virtue and this mighty Sword of Truth. These weapons will triumph over evil."

Armed with his sword and shield, the prince rushed out to find his princess. As the prince tried to escape Maleficent's domain, he had to overcome many dangers created by the evil fairy. He dodged arrows, lightning bolts, and falling rocks. But no matter what the angry Maleficent put in his way, the prince was determined to rescue Princess Aurora.

As Phillip neared the palace of King Stefan, Maleficent created a wall of thorns to stop him. But the prince hacked away at the thorny branches with the Sword of Truth until he got through.

The Prince and Samson sped toward the castle bridge.

"No!" cried Maleficent in a rage. Then, with a blinding explosion of fire, she created one last obstacle.

There before him stood the most hideous black beast he had ever seen. It was Maleficent! She had turned herself into a fierce fire-breathing dragon!

"Now you shall deal with me!" the beast cried.

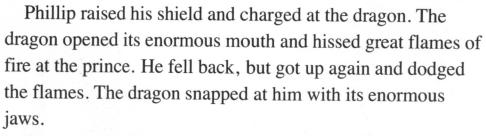

Phillip raised his shield and charged at the dragon. The dragon opened its enormous mouth and hissed great flames of fire at the prince. He fell back, but got up again and dodged the flames. The dragon snapped at him with its enormous jaws.

The prince turned and tried to retreat, but he found himself cornered on the edge of a cliff. The fairies watched anxiously, terrified for his life.

The prince raised his shield, but the dragon's hot breath knocked it into the abyss below. The dragon was ready to finish the prince with a final blast of flame.

The prince threw his Sword of Truth with all his might. It flew straight into the dragon's heart. The beast reared back, then plunged over the edge of the cliff into the darkness below.

Now the path to King Stefan's castle was clear. Phillip mounted Samson and rode through the castle gates past the sleeping guards and guests and servants.

He followed the three fairies up a winding staircase to the tower chamber where Aurora lay asleep. He approached the bed and gently kissed the sleeping princess.

Aurora opened her eyes and smiled. Instantly everyone in the castle began to awaken, too.

"Now, you were saying, Hubert...." yawned King Stefan.

"Ah, yes," King Hubert continued. "My son Phillip says he's going to marry...."

But before King Hubert could finish explaining that his son was going to marry a peasant girl, the trumpets sounded. All eyes turned to the grand staircase, where Princess Aurora and Prince Phillip made their entrance, arm in arm.

"It's Aurora! She's here!" cried King Stefan.

It was a very joyous reunion as the king and queen welcomed their daughter after sixteen long years. With open arms, Aurora ran to her parents. All fears were now gone. Maleficent was dead.

King Hubert tried to ask Phillip about the peasant girl he wanted to marry.

"What does this mean, boy?" he asked. But before he could find out, Aurora stepped up to the king and gave him a big kiss. He blushed with pleasure.

Then it was announced that the prince and princess wished to marry. The two kings were overjoyed. Their kingdoms would be united at last.

Then Phillip and Aurora danced together as the kings and the Queen and all their subjects looked on. It was indeed a joyous celebration.

The three good fairies watched the festivities from a balcony above.

"I just love happy endings," Fauna said with a sigh. And they all agreed that this was certainly the happiest of endings.

This edition produced for
Longmeadow Press
by Twin Books Corp

ISBN 0-681-41432-4

Printed in Hong Kong